ASYA PEKUROVSKAYA

First Book of the First Series

Spark, the Stone Man

Illustrated by Olga Titova

Pekasus
Factory of Animated Dreams

Don't open new worlds, open your eyes!

Published by Pekasus, 2011

Written by Asya Pekurovskaya
Edited by Peter Kovalsky
Illustrated by Olga Titova
Layout by Valentine Pavlovsky

e-mail: Pekasus2011@gmail.com

tel.: 1 (650) 681-9703 (USA), tel.: + 49 7632 823011 (Germany), tel.: + 7 (499) 781-4608 (Moscow)

www.an-animation.com

ISBN: 978-0-9828487-1-5
Library of Congress Control Number 2010911130

Spark The Stone Man.
First Book of the First Series

Stone Man, a dreamer, descends from the top of the austere Granite Mountain into a luxurious valley
where an amazing world awaits him with magic secrets, vibrant sensations, and daring ordeals.

Many thanks to Serge Shats for inauguration.

Boundless gratitude to Aida Zyablikova for her relentless participation, for criticism and encouragement. Without her this book would have never been written.

To Stella

Sand and Granite

No matter where the morning wind blew in from, no matter how it hurried along, passing the clouds by, it was sure to turn into Lemon Drop Valley, bringing with it echoes of news, smells of the battlefield and pinches of magical herbs.

Lemon Drop Valley was a place where there hung on the air itself a light and luminous haze that bestowed tranquility, not only to the kindhearted Yushkas and Pyzhiks, but also to the crude aborigines, the Klots.

At the crack of dawn the Yushkas were already crowded at the seashore, bending over a minor-like basin to perform their unchanging morning ritual before heading off to work at the weaving factory.

But what exactly was Lemon Drop Valley?

From a bird's eye view it resembled a boat, squeezed between a mountain range on the east and the gently sloping seaside on the west.

The beach was covered with waves of soft sand, so yellow that lemon drops immediately spring to mind.

Walking on the warm sand, it was hard to imagine that crossing the Valley from west to east would leave you resting against the rigid spine of the cold Granite Mountain.

That spine resembled a castle made of transparent, icy droplets that, piling up one on top of another, formed the pointed walls and towers.

And all of this glittered in the light of the sun, but on foggy days it threatened to crash down and bury the entire Valley and all its blossoming splendor.

"Who would dare to climb its hostile and icy face?" the Valley folk thought to themselves, fully confident that Granite Mountain was as lifeless as a desert.

And how could they think otherwise, having never seen a single inhabitant of Granite Mountain with their own eyes?

When the wizard Lestro told tales of the stonemasons who worked with their picks to turn boulders into dwellings, furniture, bowls and plates, and even blankets and pillows, they found it hard to believe. In their wildest fantasies, there was no room for the thought that pillows and blankets could be made out of stone.

Of course, the time would come when they would be convinced that the glacial spine of Granite Mountain was indeed the Royal Palace, for it was clearly there that the adventures of Spark, the stone man of the stonemasons' tribe had begun.

He was called Spark or, to be precise... Spark was the name to which he responded.

One might ask: what's the use of a name to which no one responds?

Well, in addition to the names to which they responded (called "twittering" names on Granite Mountain), the stonemasons also had secret names, the meanings of which could be revealed in their deeds — that is, in their heroic pursuits.

When a stonemason accomplished a heroic deed, he was allowed to modify his twittering name by adding a letter from his secret one. And only the old King of Granite Mountain had a twittering name that coincided with his secret one.

His name was Misparko-Para-Sol-Spark-Ling. That's how many glorious deeds he'd performed in the course of his life!

Of course, before count could be kept of Spark's acts of bravery, he had to grow up a little.

"Just wait until you are older..." the stonemasons would say to encourage him...

And although Spark didn't like to think about things that had yet to happen (he called them "coral fantasies," as they popped in on him only at the Coral stone), one such fantasy literally traveled with him. He fancied himself a sculptor. That is, he still imagined himself being Spark, but this new Spark already knew how to work with a real chisel.

"But where did this fantasy come from?" you may ask.

From birth, Spark had had a knack for chiseling toys out of precious minerals — silly droplets, cubes and pyramids — which he arranged on a stone ledge, making it look as festive as a Christmas tree.

Once, when he was in His Majesty's castle, he saw an unmoving figure made of stone.

"Who are you?" he asked the figure.

"This is a statue. A work by a sculptor," a passing stonemason said to him.

"What is a statue? Is it different from a stonemason?"

"Just wait until you are older..." the stonemason replied mysteriously.

And so Spark waited.

He grew with all his might, sitting on the edge of a cliff. But when his body grew and became stronger, he saw himself resembling stonemasons and, incidentally, all of them at once. But he wanted to be Spark and Spark alone.

And it was then that a wild fantasy took hold of him.

With a stone pillow under his head, he started to dream of Lemon Drop Valley. He would fall asleep every evening holding in his mind the same image of himself coming to the edge of Granite Mountain, pushing himself into the air and...

You cannot imagine how bold and how dangerous this fantasy was! According to the laws of stonemasons, even the desire to set foot beyond the cold stone of Granite Mountain was treason.

And Spark felt himself a traitor every time he went to bed harboring his secret thoughts of exploring Lemon Drop Valley.

"Now I am flying downwards, hurtling through the air!" he fantasized. But what's next? What does this Valley look like? Perhaps it's icy like a skating rink, or prickly like a cactus! Or, better, yet...

"Let there be not a single stone in this Valley! Let me walk barefoot upon the warm earth! And should there be no warm earth in the Valley, let it have lots and lots of soft sand! For surely, there is no shortage of sand anywhere in the world!"

So, Spark dreamt the sand, so bright that it dazzled him — and perhaps not only him. And no sooner could he take a step than his foot would leave its indelible, its inimitable mark. Oh, how delightful was that dream!

"Delightful, delightful," he would repeat in his sleep until he woke with the sad realization that his magnificent adventure had been nothing more than a fantasy.

Secret of the Three

One day Spark fell asleep by the icy palace of His Majesty the King, where sleeping was decidedly forbidden. Yet instead of being punished, he benefited from it.

That is certainly not to say that he received a reward of any sort. It means simply that he discovered a mystery so grand that it made his wildest fantasies seem trifling and mundane by comparison.

It is time for you to learn that the King of the stonemasons was very old. He was more than a hundred years of age, and due to this was no longer able to chisel the laws in the Holy Book. And this meant, clearly, that he couldn't rule his Kingdom anymore.

Yet the Kingdom, as I am sure you will agree, must be ruled! Moreover, it must be ruled every day, every hour and even every minute. What to do?

So, the Chief vizier found a solution. He proposed that the King appoint him the Royal double.

"But you do not look a bit like me," the King protested. "And besides, one can't become a double! A double is born a double, or he's no double at all!"

"This isn't quite so, Your Majesty," the vizier responded. "If you start thinking of me as your double, and I start thinking of you as my double, we will surely become one another's double. Mind over matter!"

"And yet I am not quite sure how to convince my subjects that you are me and I am you," the King pondered.

"A piece of cake," the vizier laughed. "All you have to do is start your day by bringing the King's crown to me on a cushion made of amethyst."

The argument was so convincing that without delay, the old King ordered an extra mantle made, with a cape of emeralds. But to distinguish himself from his Royal double, His Majesty requested that one emerald be cut off and replaced with a crystal.

And all of this was to be kept secret.

And because it had been believed from the beginning of time that crystal could both exist and not exist at the same time, all this would have gone unnoticed, had not Spark been in the Royal Palace at just that moment...

But how, you might ask, could Spark find himself in the Royal Palace? Why would he have access to His Majesty's Throne Room?

Well, on top of Granite Mountain, where little Spark grew up, there was nothing but unassailable cliffs and stones, with the exception of a single crooked maple tree, its roots drawing what life they could from the barren cliff face.

A tree growing out of a cliff? Hard to believe, yes, but true! Sometimes it even produced a sticky maple syrup that the stonemasons collected to sweeten their tea.

Next to that crooked maple tree, there stood a huge coral colored slab called the Coral stone, and it had a rather remarkable property.

No matter where little Spark fell asleep (and he fell asleep in a lot of strange places, since he loved to run and play among the stones until he found a comfortable spot to lie down), he would always wake up on the Coral stone. Even harder to believe, yes, but just as true!

This time, however, things turned out differently.

Having fallen asleep on the Coral stone, Spark woke up right under the windows of His Majesty's Throne Room. And the Throne Room was well lit — so well lit that little Spark could press his face against the icy windowpanes and, despite the dark and moonless night, make out, through the ice panels, the two Kings.

"Two Kings can't be in one place at the same time!" Spark exclaimed.

Fearing that his eyes were playing tricks on him, Spark picked a corner of the window and started breathing on it to melt the ice. It wasn't long before he'd melted a little hole in the window.

Of course, by making such a hole in the Royal window, he broke the law protecting the sanctity of His Majesty's icy palace. And that was bad. But at the same time, he acquired a privilege he could hardly have dreamed of: he could hear the two Kings' conversation as clearly as if he had been invited to the Throne Room as an honorary adviser. And that was so wonderful that it balanced everything out.

"Today
I will hand over
the Royal Scepter to you,
and you will become the ruler
of Granite Mountain," said the
coarse voice of His Majesty.

And the King bowed his gray-haired
head in silence, holding his Royal Scepter
next to his heart.

Spark understood perfectly well why the King
so revered his Royal Scepter. It was a long rod of
18 carat gold, in the upper part of which a flower
bloomed in splendor, its petals made out of
precious stones: sapphires, diamonds and pearls.

"Along with the Royal Scepter," the King continued after a long pause, "you will receive power over the stonemason's souls. But before I hand this mighty instrument of power to you, I must reveal a secret that is not known to a single soul in my Kingdom."

The King grew silent again. And Spark who had been entranced by the Royal Scepter only a moment before, now almost forgot about it.

The secret, unknown to anyone in the whole of Granite Mountain, commanded his full attention now.

However, the King, it seemed, changed his mind and withdrew into silence. Yet Spark was so eager to learn the secret that he almost called out, urging His Majesty to hurry up with the news.

Fortunately, he was able to contain himself. And for that he was amply rewarded. The secret that followed was worth a little suffering.

"There is an entrance to Lemon Drop Valley called 'the Coveted Path' hidden under the Coral stone near the crooked maple tree," the King finally said, pointing his Royal Scepter in the direction where little Spark was hiding.

Spark couldn't believe his ears.

"Lemon Drop Valley will cease to be just a dream for me from now on!" he thought with delight.

"I knew it! Oh, yes, I could even predict it! Now the stonemasons will rush to the Valley, all at once! In fact, I see them moving along as we speak!" the indignant Royal double bewailed. He must have already thought himself to be the real King. "Now just try and stop them!"

"But why do you say: 'as we speak,' my dear vizier? The secret is not known to anyone, but you." His Majesty retorted.

However, His Majesty's retort had no effect on the Royal vizier.

"When the law loses its power," he continued, "and I can sense it starting to lose its power even now, its subjects will become unruly and abandon Granite Mountain, and we will be condemned to win our daily bread by hewing the cliffs ourselves. Oh, woe is us! Woe is us!"

While the vizier was painting the devastating picture of the fall of the Royal House, the King was silent. His Majesty didn't break the silence even when the vizier collapsed into an armchair and covered his face with his hands.

"But the main secret is something else," the old King finally said, standing erect and leaning on his Royal Scepter. "The main secret begins with the fact that we all," His voice sounded so solemn that Spark felt a shiver down his spine, "that all stonemasons," the King clarified, "are born with iron shoes to protect their stone soles..."

The King grew silent again, and the Chief vizier was bewildered, not daring to ask the question that was ready to drop from the tip of his tongue. He simply could not understand what the iron shoes, the iron shoes that every stonemason polished before he went to work in the morning, had to do with secrets. But he didn't say a word, fearing to appear ill-informed before his King.

"Well, the main secret is," His Majesty spoke again, "that the Coveted Path has been magnetized since the time of the Inventors! And when the Inventors left the Valley, no one could demagnetize that path — no one but the Great wizard Lestro, who lives in the hollow of the Old Valley Oak."

The King had said all that he had to say and his vizier fell to his knees, speaking the words of an oath.

"I'll find the Wizard! I'll convince him that our King deserves to rule free of worries! The hollow of the Old Valley Oak!"

The Lemon Drop Valley

"The hollow of the Old Valley Oak," repeated little Spark to himself not quite knowing that these simple words would forever change the course of his life.

Can you imagine that it hadn't even occurred to him that this journey (to which he devoted much thought each day) might cost him his life. And when the thought of consequences did enter his mind, he said to himself, "If I allowed myself to be frightened by every dangerous thought that comes to my mind, I would already have died many times over."

But it is one thing to set your mind to do something dangerous, and quite another to really do it. For to start upon a journey, even one not so risky as this, it is necessary to work out a plan.

And if you have never worked out a plan in your entire life, you'll be sure to encounter some unexpected obstacles.

For example, Spark noticed that his thoughts had started to become entangled with his dreams, and he would sometimes interrupt his own thoughts, fearful that he was merely dreaming them...

Spark was convinced that he knew the Coral stone like the back of his hand, and should there be any path there, he would have noticed it one way or the other. But then he interrupted himself, suddenly irresolute. And he wanted to run to the Coral stone to find out for sure whether or not the Coveted Path was indeed there.

But even this impulse was tempered by a new fear: "What if someone notices me moving the Coral stone?"

As you can see, the plan didn't come to Spark so easily.

Finally he decided to postpone descending to the Valley till a day when the stonemasons locked the doors of their dwellings, which they do, strangely enough, on sunny days.

So, for a sunny day he waited.

Luckily, he didn't have to wait long.

The very next day he woke up feeling the sweetness of the sun's warmth. And without waiting for the sun's disk to rise from behind the mountains, Spark hurried to confirm that the Coveted Path did indeed exist.

"Bingo!" Spark whispered when he found the path and rushed into the Valley.

To say that he "rushed," however, doesn't exactly describe his action, for as soon as he took his first step on the sheer cliff, he had the strange sensation that his legs were being weighed down as if they had grown into the cliff itself, yet his body became weightless, giving itself to soaring on the air.

"How wonderful it is to be free!" he cried out, then promptly silenced himself so as not to disclose the secret of the Coveted Path.

"How wonderful it is to be free!" reverberated the echo, and Spark slid slowly down the steep cliff, which seemed to him no more difficult than a flat skating rink. The Coveted Path magically held him such that he could move slowly while at the same time covering vast distances.

His journey lasted almost the whole day.

When Spark found himself at the foot of Granite Mountain and stepped onto the ground, it literally embraced him with its soft warmth.

It was Lemon Drop Valley, offering its first greeting to its visitor.

Not without reason do they say that once you've set foot in the Valley, you will never wish to leave it behind. And Spark felt exactly that when he found himself under the cupola of a magical greenhouse.

No sooner had he taken a few steps when some yellow-orange hibiscuses with red hearts settled on his shoulders, touching him tenderly with their heads. He tried to wiggle out of them and immediately felt the breath of the vibrant yuccas that placed their little white bells before him. And even though he tread rather carefully, still he couldn't avoid disturbing some of the "living stones" which were in fact minuscule plants all white and yellow. Next, some yellow mimosas appeared in clusters and prickly cacti protruded from the earth next to them, whose bites Spark hardly even noticed.

The sweet, heady, suffocating odor of life itself enveloped him!
Still stupefied by all the spicy floral smells, Spark started
to look for a way out of this splendid greenhouse when,
suddenly, yet another new sight took his breath away.

Two moons stared down at him, unblinking.

He promptly rubbed his eyes, but to no avail. Two circular disks, each an exact replica of the other, still glowed on the horizon like two vigilant eyes.

One moon — and he could see it clearly — was mild and flowing as if it were made out of wax, yet the other...

No, he could not get a good look at the other moon until he had stepped into the square, which was also the beginning of a promenade.

You have to bear in mind that neither the square nor the promenade quite deserved their names.

The promenade was a path that ran along the high seaside, attracting some dressed-up Valley folk who liked to stroll about, to posture and puff themselves up, and, in short, to show off. The square, on the other hand, was a round place above which a statue of some famous person or another, in whose honor the monument had been erected, held a shining, sparkling crystal ball.

And no sooner had Spark stepped into the round square that he saw that the crystal ball was, indeed, the second moon that he had only glimpsed before. The ball would glow all night, lighting up at the hour of the actual moon's rising, and mimic all it's shades and colors until the dawn.

And the magician's hat sitting on the statue's head left no doubt that you were indeed facing a wizard, and not just any wizard, but rather the Great wizard Lestro who would one day open an unimagined world of sorcery and magic to Spark.

"It's a good thing you don't look like a stonemason!" Spark thought joyfully.

Yet just as he opened his mouth to speak his thoughts, he saw Klot the giant approaching him from out of the darkness.

Of course Spark withdrew in fear, and rightly so, for as soon as the Klot came level with the monument, both moons disappeared and it became dark and scary.

But then, Spark heard a song.

All our furniture, I noted,
Left us, giving no notice.
Beds broke free in flying leaps.
So, where should we sleep?

Our beautiful buffet
Thrown somewhere else its fête.
Poor Klots are simply doomed
Puzzling over what to do.

And even though Klot the giant sang in a deep bass, Spark no longer felt afraid at all. Moreover, he found it rather amusing that such a huge creature could turn out to be such a helpless complainer.

Spark's conversation with the monument, however, had to be postponed. The presence of a giant, even one not so scary, but still a total stranger, didn't leave Spark inclined to a friendly chat. Besides, he had more of Lemon Drop Valley to explore.

On the Promenade

As soon as Spark left the square, he found himself on the promenade, and it didn't take him long to see that it had earned its name.

The dressed up Valley folk were indeed promenading on it. And the very first pair strolling by struck Spark as utterly stunning.

The beau's name, as Spark was about to discover, was Super-Pyzhik. Or, rather, he inherited the name from a legendary ancestor who had created a magical substance that put an end to the long war between the Pyzhiks and the Volchaks.

This descendant, too, seemed to deserve the glorious name of Super-Pyzhik.

He walked grandly, throwing forward his long stork-like legs clad in green boots, his head decorated with a green silk hat. In his mouth he held a clay pipe, and on one eye he wore a gold-rimmed monocle.

It was hard to imagine how one could move so gracefully, keeping all these accessories in balance, while carrying on the most captivating conversation.

But that wasn't the whole of it.

Super-Pyzhik spoke, stretching his words like a rubber band, puffing on his clay pipe and occasionally running ahead of his companion, Stella the Yushka, to look into her eyes.

"To some pe-ee-ople, it's simply not gi-ii-ven to kno-oow of true wizards' treasures. For a wizard wouldn't displa-aa-y his real possessi-oo-ns, just to sho-oow-offois!"

"Wow, you've mixed up some letters," Stella interrupted him. "Did you mean to say, 'to show off'?"

"Why would I say 'to show off-ois', if I had meant to say 'to show off'?"

"Well, it's possible to say what you don't mean or to mean what you don't say. They are not the same at all," Stella retorted.

"Why not? When I say that to vi-ii-sit the Great wizard's ca-aa-stle you must possess a go-oo-ld trimmed envelo-oo-pe with a m-oo-nogram in the shape of the letter 'L', illu-uu-minated with golden oo-ak leaves, don't I think the very same thing?"

Of course, Super-Pyzhik's confidence stemmed from the fact that, both in his thought and in his manner, he strove to resemble one of wizard Lestro's honorable guests. And he had no choice in the matter because of how badly he wanted to impress the beautiful Stella.

What a charming creature she was! Her fluffy white fur stood up porcupine-style, and from her head grew a shoulder-length dreadlock tied with a blue ribbon. She was clad in a blue velvet dress, and in her hands she carried a pair of blue high-heeled shoes. Everything about her was sylph-like and airy and undeniably irresistible. But most mesmerizing was her lovely neck, over which a grey silk scarf was casually thrown.

And if you also consider her magical talents, it comes as no surprise that near her, not only Super-Pyzhik, but even little Spark, a casual passerby, felt utterly out of place.

So, Spark was all the more surprised by what happened next! How could he imagine that splendid Super-Pyzhik would be so embarrassed!

His monocle, which until a moment ago had seemed to be an inalienable part of his magnificence, leaped from his face and vanished, along with its golden rim.

How flustered poor Super-Pyzhik looked when he fell to his knees and began to rummage around in the embarrassing position ordinarily called "on all fours."

On the face of it, it looked hilarious. But luckily for Super-Pyzhik, Stella was distracted by thoughts of even greater importance.

"Who needs this envelope? I bet the wizard will welcome us without standing on ceremony, and will grant a full country mile of my wishes. And even Mash-fatum will serve at my feet," Stella carried on. "But if you do insist on getting it for me, why don't you hire a footman in livery?"

Well, the moment came for Super-Pyzhik to respond. He had to act decisively, lest he aggravate his clumsy situation. So, he sprung back to his feet, abandoning his monocle (which, incidentally, Spark picked up, intending to return it to its owner when an opportunity presented itself).

"Exactly! A foo-oo-tman... there is none better trained in the great art of delivering g-oo-ld-trimmed envel-oo-pes!" Super-Pyzhik hurriedly asserted with ceremonious dignity.

Needless to say that although Spark stayed on the promenade following the ravishing couple until they vanished from his sight, he failed to bring to fruition his good intention — to return the monocle to its rightful owner — and to free himself of the thoughts that had captured his imagination.

"Well! Not only the Great wizard, but also some mysterious Mash-fatum are hiding in the hollow of the Old Valley Oak," Spark thought, contemplating off-handedly what his first wish would be. "I wish to be the messenger, in golden livery, versed in the great art of delivering gold-trimmed envelopes, destined to bring just such an envelope to Stella... though, I suppose I could do without the livery."

As soon as Spark could clarify his first thought, he could already throw himself into the boldest speculations.

"If he had doubted that such a place existed, the Royal vizier would never have promised to find Lestro in the hollow of the Old Valley Oak. And if such a place exists, someone has to know where it is. But who?"

This is what little Spark thought to himself, never suspecting that both the great Lestro's and the King's mailman was none other than the wind. And how upset he was when he finally learned that not a single soul in the Valley knew where to find the hollow of the Old Valley Oak. Even the birds flew right past it and built their nests at a distance.

But little Spark wasn't ready to give up yet.

He thought and he thought until something dawned on him.

"It's simply impossible that a wizard can do without guests! And as guests are normally more numerous than their hosts, they are easier to find. But one needs to meet them when they are least prepared — that is, when they are on the way to pay their host a visit."

The Viscount's Boot

So, Spark began to wander around the Valley, trying to imagine what Lestro's guest might look like.

The guest of a wizard, he can't look ordinary. He ought to be dressed up, looking like he has nothing whatsoever to do...

Of course, it was not such an easy thing to find someone who has absolutely nothing to do in Lemon Drop Valley. No one seemed to look particularly busy, so every passerby could be taken for one of Lestro's guests. But when Spark finally came across one, all his doubts vanished and he knew his search was over.

"That's him!"

Later, Spark learned that the grand gentleman, who was indeed the Great wizard's guest, came from Paris and bore the honorable title of Viscount.

But for now, Lestro's guest was the one (obviously with no advance warning, or any warning at all, for that matter) who would lead our little adventurer to the castle of the Great wizard.

The Viscount's splendid outfit was abundant with folds, creases, foamy lace, pockets and cuffs of various sorts. His knee-high boots were adorned with, in addition to buckles and lapels, some leather loops and shoestrings. And, if you can believe it, at the end of one of the shoestrings was a brass plate with some words engraved upon it, being dragged behind him like a train.

It was these shoestrings that our resourceful Spark picked up and quickly attached to his own leg. And that was prudent, for no sooner had he finished his preparation when the Viscount took a few big, sweeping steps, forcing Spark to run after him.

That was the way they moved along for some time, until some magic force lifted both, carrying them high through the air. But once the pair took off, Spark realized that he had made one rather annoying mistake.

Having tied his leg to the Viscount's boot, he found himself flying upside down. And since it was too late to fix anything, he was dizzy for the duration of the flight. He was particularly uncomfortable when they ran across some potholes: and while entering the oak's hollow, he bumped painfully against its side. Only when his guide started to slow, gliding along the rounded surface of the hollow and then sliding down along a soft, moss path did Spark feel like himself again.

But at just that moment, the Viscount was blinded by the radiance of the burning rays of the sun and came to a sudden halt, as if he had applied some invisible brakes.

Later, Spark learned that the radiance was not of the sun at all. It was a cloud of golden fireflies that filled the entrance to the cave like heavy blinds.

But when Spark took his first step into the cave, together with the Viscount, with whom he had become one, a new wonder awaited him.

In the middle of the cave there grew a solitary castle. Yes, grew, not stood. It grew, just as cake grows in the oven or seaweed grows in the sea.

Each year the castle sprouted a few new tooth-like towers, and it had been growing for so many years that it now looked like a tree stump covered with mushrooms.

But who in his right mind could call the wizard's dwelling a tree stump?

It was indeed a castle, with all the proper attributes of a castle. Though it's true that it wasn't as gloomy and passionless as many of them are, and it didn't seem quite as desolate due, perhaps, to the fact that its windows were illuminated by thousands of chandeliers.

Finally the journey ended. Just one more moment and Spark would step into the Wizard's home!

"What's happening? Am I not done with my flight?" The thought flared through Spark's mind.

It so happened that the Viscount had taken off his knee-high boots, giving no warning to anyone, and, with a single swing, threw them onto a hook that was attached to the chimney.

And little Spark was hanging upside down again, bumping painfully against the wall. Only this time, the torture seemed destined to last forever.

As soon as he got accustomed to being suspended, Spark started to notice the things around him. For example, he spotted two more hooks upon which hung some odd objects, which turned out to be footware of kinds that Spark could never have imagined. Never in his entire life had he seen shoes made of anything other than stone. With astonishment, he gazed at sandals with leather straps, taken from the foot of an Indian magician from Kerala, and also at some soft, silk embroidered slippers that belonged to a follower of Confucius from Shanghai.

"Ah, Viscount Pierre, I am so happy that you are here," said a soft voice from the ground.

Glancing down, Spark noticed a creature, standing with its head up.

"If he's talking to me, why did he call me some Viscount?" Spark thought, irritated.

"Can't you make yourself useful instead of just gawking at me? Don't you see I am in trouble?" he remarked rather rudely.

But no sooner had he made this ill-mannered remark than he noticed the brass plate attached to his leg on which was written: "I, Viscount Pierre, am here."

Of course, Spark had no way of knowing that these words had been written by Pierre's mother, blessing her son on a dangerous journey. But at least now Spark understood why the stranger had addressed him as "Viscount Pierre."

"Well, you were mistaken, Viscount Pierre... I wasn't just staring at you! I simply thought you were hanging because you had nothing better to do."

"I'm the one with nothing better to do?" demanded Spark indignantly.

"If you are engaged in some worthwhile endeavor, I beg your pardon — I must have failed to notice," the voice from below replied politely.

"What worthwhile thing could I possibly be doing, hanging here like this?"

"I am overjoyed that you've got some free time! Allow me to introduce myself: I am Tonino the Medun; I deliver pastries to the wizard. See?"

Tonino proudly lifted a package over his head. "But now, please, excuse me. I am afraid I am almost running late!"

"What?! Do you really plan to just leave me hanging here?" Spark cried indignantly.

"Good Heavens, no! I will surely come back soon, Viscount Pierre! Keep it a little while, if you please!

"It's easy to say: 'keep it a little while'!" Spark managed to yell after him.

But Tonino the Medun had disappeared, and for some time Spark could still see his timid smile, even though all his life he had believed that a smile couldn't exist all by itself, but always belonged to whomever was smiling.

Lestro's Guests

Even when he had devised a plan for freeing himself, having begun thinking of such a plan immediately after Tonino's disappearance, Spark knew that had Tonino not left his smile behind, the plan would have been doomed to fail.

"I shall swing on this cord as long as it takes to break it!" he decided and took action. First, he pushed himself off the wall and swung up. Then he pushed off harder and swung up again. This time he swung so high that he could have looked into Lestro's open window, had he managed to grab onto it. But he missed the right moment, and only on the third attempt was he able to see what was inside.

Lestro was sitting silently at the head of a long table, set for four, and observing his guests, who were also withdrawn into silence.

"I'm glad I didn't miss anything! Had the conversation started, it wouldn't have stopped until the farewell at the door," Spark thought and availed himself of the opportunity to observe.

The Great wizard Lestro painted some symbols in the air, and pots of steaming food, chilled decanters of wine and a crystal bowl full of fresh vegetables flew through the air.

Supper was unassuming: pumpkin soup, Caesar Salad and, as a tribute to the east, Shishkebab Ambary with lamb, and Prawns Malabar with mushroom mousse.

"Gentlemen," the Confucian from Shanghai broke the silence, poking his salad with his fork, "I asked you to gather here for a good cause. My confidential sources tell me that a secret society in Foggy Albion Valley is preparing the World Fire."

"I'll be darned!" cried out the Indian magician from Kerala, swallowing a mouthful of lamb. "In some ways, I suspected that! A sect has appeared in Kerala..." Then he shut his eyes, keeping them closed for so long that Spark started to wonder whether or not he had fallen asleep.

Yet at the moment when Spark decided that the guest had simply resolved to relax a bit, the Indian magician's third green eye brightened and directed a stern and piercing gaze at everyone present.

"They have built fireplaces; and they light them not with a lighter, as one does in the civilized world, but with an enormous tinderbox. And from a tinderbox to a wildfire, as you understand..."

"Certainly," replied the follower of Confucius, with one leap having flown to the center of the drawing room. He folded his palms, made a polite bow, and then gave a menacing glance at all present, apparently remembering something disturbing. "I was told," he went on with a threatening whisper, and lifted high his leg, bent at the knee.

It appeared to Spark that at that moment the Confucian turned into a tiger with flailing paws. Then he lowered his leg, graciously stepping first to his heel and then to his toe. At that point his body turned into a silver-scaled dragon that looked straight into Spark's eyes.

"I was told," he continued, at the next moment transforming himself into a snake, "that wandering shades have been seen on the Great Wall of China. They appear at night, carrying baskets on their backs, and on each basket is written a character from the Ancient Book of Changes. I would like to know what they are thinking and understand the meaning of the character, which everyone has long since forgotten how to read." At that point he sat down, looking expressively at the Viscount.

The Viscount stood jerkily and kissed his sword ceremoniously after pulling it out of its sheath.

"My fa-a-therland," he said, "was also no-oo-t without some distressing signa-a-ls."

"Oh, he must be the one Super-Pyzhik is imitating," Spark observed staring at the Viscount.

"Barges sta-a-rted running into one ano-o-ther in our ha-aa-rbor. And when the investigati-oo-n was fi-ii-nished, it became cle-ee-ar that a manuscript had captiva-aa-ted all Parisians including even the ba-a-rgemen, if you can believe it: it was a list of Ro-u-yal dishes for the Tenth of Fructido-o-re. And what is crucial here is that all of Pa-aa-ris had read the sa-ee-me menu-u a week befo-oo-re King Louis XVI lo-oo-st his head."

"All these events," summarized the follower of Confucius having slurped from the cup of coffee that had just materialized in front of him, "leave us in no doubt about the credibility of Pythagoras' predictions! A universal conflagration is being prepared!"

"Nothing less than a universal conflagration?" asked Lestro.

"I hope," the Keralian replied to him, "that you will agree to bring the Great Mash-fatum out of its retirement."

"Well, has Pythagoras already come up with a plan for it?" Lestro asked, holding onto his smile.

"We don't even need a plan if we can quench the World Fire with a World Flood," said the Confucian nervously. "Can Mash-fatum complete such a simple task?"

"But why should we wait for a World Fire? Wouldn't it be safer to prevent it?" Lestro asked calmly.

"Certainly," the Keralian supported him, "we should get rid of lighters and tinderboxes. Would it be possible to ask Mash-fatum to turn lighters... into... mmm... cockroaches, and tinderboxes into flowerpots?"

"No, I'm afraid that li-ii-ving with cockroa-a-ches is si-ii-mply unacceptable!" said the Viscount resolutely. "I thi-ii-nk it would be much better to cre-ee-ate a world of confu-u-sion. Why can't we call 'lighters'... 'gliders'? That wa-aa-y any thou-u-ght of 'fire' will be replaced by thou-u-ghts of 'flying machine'. And we should rename 'menu' as well... Can we call it 'Coo-o-k's travel guide' instead? And as so-oo-on as everyone starts tra-aa-veling, who'll have time to think about Revolu-u-tions or World Fires?"

"Darn right," said all guests in unison.

"Oh, I am really vexed, my friends, for I was about to offer you something from my menu," said the wizard Lestro with a smile.

At that point, Tonino appeared before the guests, wearing a culinary cap, and Spark took note of Tonino nearly touching the floor with his snow-white headgear when he bowed.

Then Tonino handed a box to the wizard Lestro that contained a candy cane and a little poem.

> We are bringing for the nonce
> Lemon-and-banana... pudding...
> Don't confuse it with a sconce!

As Spark was wondering how words could be put together in such whimsical ways, Tonino appeared before the Viscount with a new line:

> This is not a bland crème puff!
> Please, don't spill it on your... sofa
> Or your spotless, laced-up cuff!

The Confucian, too, received his dessert with a little poem:

> Relish our apple tart,
> To create it was too... easy.
> Don't presume it was not hard!

The recipient of the last dessert was the Indian magician. Yet when Tonino handed his box to him, there was a sheep sitting in his place and fixing a napkin around its neck.

In total confusion, Tonino mumbled under his nose.

> Don't reject, for pity's sake,
> Our yummy... oatmeal porridge...
> Tastes as good as carrot cake!

Still holding the box in his hands, Tonino raised his eyes and saw the Indian magician, who was now sitting on the table in the Lotus pose.

Tonino felt utterly lost. And when Lestro's guests rushed to extend their gratitude to him (though it was not him, but Medun the Senior, who was behind these poems and these recipes) he was thinking of one thing: how to cut and run.

Yet since under no circumstance could he sacrifice his good manners, he couldn't leave without a farewell line, which he quickly concocted.

> If I were Medun the Daddy,
> I'd have taken all the credit,
> But as I am Medun the tyro...
> I fear I must... vamoose,
> Which is to say 'retire'...

With this he bowed hastily, this time really dirtying the tip of his white cap.

Spark's Dream

When he spoke of a pressing concern, of course, Tonino meant the matter of rescuing Spark. Yet even if he had forgotten about Spark entirely, there would be no one to reproach him.

Spark's thoughts were soaring rather far away. They were so far that even the Indian magician's transformations passed him by, unnoticed.

Suddenly he felt that he was no longer holding on to the fireplace pipe, but, while sitting on the Coral stone, lost himself in a coral fantasy: a huge pendulum descended before his eyes, the beautiful Stella swinging on it, clad in her blue dress and a high hair style that resembled a pyramid.

"But what if she loses her grip and falls!" he managed to think before descending into a dream.

Granite Mountain disappeared and, as though someone had simply changed the decorations, a deserted town grew in its place with a tall town wall and the gates guarded by mounted soldiers in armor.

"Can't you see that I am here on the orders of the king, Sigismund the Tail-less?" Spark demanded, stopping by the gate.

He himself was not aware how he had come to know this name. The effect, however, was most amazing: the guards stood apart, clearing the path for him, and the gates flew wide open. So, a palace with a golden roof, towers and cupolas appeared in front of him.

The most astonishing thing, however, was waiting for him inside the palace.

The moment he stepped under the resounding vaults, he heard some music that led him through a number of rooms to a huge door that flew open...

On a golden throne there sat a king in a purple mantle.

This was, of course, Sigismund the Tail-less, the king of white mice. An entourage of dressed-up courtiers encircled him. Somehow it all felt very familiar to Spark.

But here was something new!

Kneeling before the King was Stella, her hands tied.

Bravely, Spark stepped forward, holding a magic sphere that had mysteriously appeared in his hands.

It was the very same sphere that was held by the monument of the Great wizard Lestro. But now, it turned up miraculously, helping Spark by reducing to ashes everyone who would dare to come close.

The mounted guards had already started bounding towards him from all sides. Eventually, they all were doomed to perish!

Only a stone's throw away, the last remaining foe sought refuge, shuffling towards the door with his retinue. Of course, it was Sigismund the Tail-less, the tyrant, and the torturer of the beautiful Stella, his Stella.

"Oh, I am so needlessly... so absurdly late, dear Stella," Spark said untying her arms. "But...er... I... lingered over that stupid gold-trimmed envelope... which lies in my pocket now... I mean... would be lying there if it were already morning... Do you mind waiting until morning?"

Stella lifted her face, looking beautiful even in tears, and Spark felt the touch of her soft, caressing little paw on his forehead.

But it wasn't Stella at all!

When he opened his eyes, he saw Tonino sitting next to him on a ladder.

"Please, forgive me, dear Viscount!" Tonino begged. "I lingered too long... Here, if I may..."

And he swiftly freed Spark, letting him climb down the steps.

"Tell me, Tonino... if things were to unfold in such a way that someone was badly in need of a gold trimmed envelope..." he started carefully.

"Ah, you need this envelope, do you? Consider it done! You might as well have it in your hands already!" Tonino announced as he fell out of sight, whispering to Spark on his way: "See you tomorrow!"

"You are always in a rush," mused Spark looking at his own hands, just in case.

But still no envelope.

Meeting Mash-fatum

By the following evening, Spark was already standing under the Great wizard Lestro's windows, impatiently awaiting the arrival of Tonino, who, for his part, seemed to be in no hurry.

When Spark was just about to knock on the door, a ladder was lowered from a window. And what happened next, happened so quickly that Spark couldn't be sure whether or not it was a dream.

Tonino rushed down the stairs and, without reassuring Spark with a word of greeting or any explanation whatsoever, quickly tied a leather belt around the little stonemason.

Bewildered, Spark soared upwards. Someone's hand pushed him through the window, and he kept rising until, finally, he landed on a chair which had been bolted to the ceiling. And waiting for him there, upon a small table, was a cup of hot chocolate and even a little cake.

Spark could never have believed that such a thing was happening to him were it not for Tonino sitting next to him, casually dangling his legs.

There was nothing unusual in the room, except for the fact that he was still suspended under the ceiling of a fairly high tower and had already polished off a whole plate of the delicious cake.

He started looking around.

Far below was a chest of cured and darkened oak, and something stood on top of it...

And as soon Spark's eyes fell on this something, his spirits lifted and he felt a strange sensation.

"Here it is, the magic Mash-fatum," Tonino whispered, "the crown of creation, once worn by some unknown Inventor. And it can grant wishes!"

45

"Any wish?" Spark wanted to ask, but paused to consider.

It was clear that Mash-fatum was capable of granting any wish, and that there were a great many wishes in Lemon Drop Valley! Spark alone had more wishes than he could count! And should one start sorting them by their individual qualities, one would have to admit that wishes could be astonishingly whimsical, most fantastic, quite contradictory and even slightly alarming.

Should Spark make up his mind and decide what he wished for most of all at just that moment...

How strange... just as he was about to put his wish into words, his thoughts broke off as if its source had completely dried out...

Yet there was nothing astonishing in it. It was just this simple: Spark had gotten distracted from Mash-fatum, having noticed a gigantic box with the word "CABINET" written on it in huge letters.

The cabinet housed glass vessels, each filled with potions that resembled a sap, resin or perhaps cornflakes. These, of course, were not sap, not resin and certainly not cornflakes.

"In there is the magic substance called Magma Gumiar: a mixture drawn from rare herbs, including the Mangorra plant," Tonino broke the silence once more.

"Now I'll ask Mash-fatum for a gold-trimmed envelope," Spark decided and started to think how best to express his wish. "Success depends on how you ask for what you desire. And this will always be so."

It was important to let Mash-fatum sense that if it were not absolutely necessary, Spark would never dare to trouble such a wonderful, such a powerful, such a...

"No, Mash-fatum doesn't look like this at all..." Spark cut himself short. "Rather it resembles an old-fashioned coffee maker, with two rooster-like feet sticking out of it and something resembling a bell-mouth sitting on its head. But what's this? From the bell-mouth extends a tube that leads to a glass stomach, and the glass stomach contains some objects that resemble springs, gears and levers..."

"Dearest Mash-fatum, give me a gold-trimmed envelope!" begged little Spark at last.

But it was too late. The wizard Lestro was now standing next to Mash-fatum. He moved one of the attachments to the left, turned over his hourglass and sat down to watch in a chair near the fireplace.

And it was remarkable — the wheels spun into motion, small levers jumped up and down, springs compressed and decompressed.

Little Spark, who had fallen under Mash-fatum's spell, felt merry again and began to fantasize.

"I wonder what would happen if I tried to grind beans in it or perhaps even make coffee?"

What happened next was something that occurs very seldom, almost never.

Before Spark could finish thinking... Or rather: before Spark could learn what happened next, he saw a small female creature in a cap holding a little pouch full of coffee beans in her hand.

"Meet Bertha the Mouse, the wizard Lestro's favorite servant," Tonino whispered to Spark.

Tale IX

Bertha's Metamorphoses

As much as Bertha revered the Great wizard, she did not think very highly of his practical skills.

"I'd like to grind coffee beans in Mash-fatum," she said quietly, throwing a mocking glance in Lestro's direction.

As you can see, Bertha the Mouse didn't deem it necessary to ask for his permission. And when she poured the contents of her pouch into the bell-mouth of the magic machine, and turned its copper hand to the right, the question of permission became irrelevant.

The magic potion boiled instantly, and something resembling a porcupine's coat bristled up; from its spines, which of course were glass tubes, clouds of smoke billowed out. Everything in the tower room came to motion: a Bohemian chandelier made of crystal began to swing, the piano lid came open, as did the door of the cage of the parrot Flaubert, releasing the prisoner, who immediately disappeared out the window frame.

Adventures awaited Bertha as well.

"Ah, help me!" she screamed.

And it seemed to her that she'd just dropped down into the bedroom of the king of white mice, Sigismund the Tail-less. But instead of His Majesty sitting on the Royal Throne, it was a fat black cat with two burning greenish-yellow eyes and a yellow bowtie. And he was waiting for her.

Bertha covered her head with her apron and promptly fainted.

"Is this really the end?" she thought. "The end! The end!" The words kept pulsing in her temples. And she could already imagine the sound of a funeral bell filling the air!

Someone was throwing her down into the grave. "Where did these characters come from? One of them must be Uncle Waldemar. Next to him is his son, what's his name... They seem to love throwing dirt at me... And who is that? Ah, that's Aunt Brunhilde... placing a yellow rose on the lid of my coffin... Is it a rose or a bell?

Of course it's a bell, and it tolls for me! Bertha thought and promptly came back to life.

To her surprise, instead of the black cat and a funeral procession, Bertha saw the wizard Lestro. Sitting in a chair, he was ringing a bell impatiently.

He was dressed in a black frock with a yellow bowtie.

Yes, had Bertha known more about the properties of Mash-fatum, she would never have dared to turn the hand of the magic mechanism, let alone turn it to the right. For it was precisely this right turn that had activated Magma Gumiar, the primary property of which is that it seeps through the skin in the form of a poison.

And this experiment could have cost Bertha her life, had she not managed to utter, at the last moment, the word "Ah," which literally means "five minutes" in the language of Gummiarabicum.

And so, without her even suspecting it, Bertha had requested a temporary death which would last precisely five minutes. And that, as you see, is exactly what happened.

It would be appropriate to mention here that thanks to her little adventure with Mash-fatum, Bertha realized what wonders the magic machine was capable of, and did not touch it again. Also, from this point on she addressed the wizard always as "the Illustrious-and-Powerful."

Can you imagine! Spark was able to see all that had happened to Bertha the Mouse, including even her dream, as clearly as if he had been sitting in front of a TV screen.

And he felt so sorry for Bertha, for she was denied help when she needed it most!

Spark strained from his chair to save her. Yet exactly at that critical moment, someone willed the belt wrapped around him to move and return him to the spot below the window where he had started.

"Some scoundrel has pulled me out of the castle!" Spark exclaimed when he found himself on the ground below Lestro's windows.

"Well, with blatant disregard for the circumstances, one could say that the scoundrel was I," Tonino replied.

That was beyond what Spark could envision.

"So it was you who prevented me from helping poor Bertha?"

"But why was it up to you to save her?"

"Because I was near... and I could commit an act of bravery in the nick of time."

"And who needs your help, when Bertha is being taken care of by the kindest and wisest wizard in the world?" countered Tonino quietly as he put a gold-trimmed envelope in Spark's hand.

The Promenade Once More

ressing the envelope to his heart, Spark couldn't imagine any-thing that might stand between him and Stella. And as he knew of no place to search for her other than the promenade...

If you think he rushed straight to the promenade, you are quite wrong!

Prior to starting the search for Stella, he had to prepare himself. And to pre-pare himself, he had to return to the dream in which he met Stella in the castle of Sigismund the Tail-less. There he had appeared before her as a hero and a savior.

And he couldn't wait to rush to Stella in order to untie her... But no, her hands won't be tied, of course, for his actual meeting with her will be on the promenade!

Now he imagined himself coming up to her and settling the issue once and for all by handing her the envelope...

"But what if I approach her from behind?" he interrupted himself.

"Then I'll most likely run ahead and then return, pretending to run into her by accident.

But what about the envelope? No, I must come up with a way to address her which will account for everything. 'We slightly know each other,' he composed in motion. '... Or, rather, I have met you before... and would have surely met you earlier, but earlier I was not where you were... regrettably... Well, you might be pleased to learn that I've gotten a gold-trimmed envelope for you. I could have waited till the morning, of course... But you were so eager to have it in your hands. Oh, I forgot to introduce myself... I am Spark!'"

Satisfied with his speech, Spark could already picture Stella leaning towards him in gratitude and even felt the touch of her soft and tender paw...

By this point, he was already walking the promenade and could not understand what he saw. There was not a single soul there.

The thought that Stella might not be where he expected her to be hadn't occurred to Spark for even a single moment.

"Perhaps she wandered over to the square?"

Yet the square was empty as well, except, of course, for the monument to Lestro, who was still holding high the shining sphere of the moon, turning pale in anticipation of the approaching morning.

Despondent, Spark walked back along the promenade, heading towards the Coveted Path. But suddenly, he heard laughter.

He looked down at the sandy beach and froze.

On Super-Pyzhik's jacket, casually thrown on the sand, sat Stella, clasping her knees with her hands. Next to her knelt Super-Pyzhik, combing her silky hair.

"Again you forget everything!" he chided her gently.

"Not everything," Stella replied with a winsome smile. "I don't recall ever mentioning any gold-trimmed envelopes, and even if I had, I am sure I was just unimaginably bored…"

Overwhelmed by what he heard, Spark rushed away, covering his face with his hands.

Then he remembered something, and took the ill-fated envelope from his pocket.

With all his remaining strength he threw the envelope away, and, unable to resist the temptation, opened his eyes to see its fate.

The wind caught the envelope and carried it out towards the sea.

Letters from Lemon Drop Valley

All the following day Spark thought about Lemon Drop Valley, which had made him so miserable.

"Maybe I should just stay here, on Granite Mountain? The stonemasons are so kind to me," Spark thought.

But a little voice stubbornly insisted that if he stayed away from Lemon Drop Valley for too long, he'd wither. And he had to admit that the voice was his own.

"Enough sulking!" Spark ordered himself. "Have you forgotten your promise to help Bertha the Mouse?"

And until he said this, he had, indeed, forgotten about it entirely.

When Spark took his seat next to Tonino again, he was astonished to see that Bertha the Mouse had mounted a little stool as if nothing happened. Having donned her glasses, she was reading a letter sent by the Royal double of the stonemasons a day earlier.

As the letter was signed "His Majesty," it was unclear who wrote it: the real King or his double. One thing removed any doubt, however — namely that the words "His Majesty," no matter where they were found, were capitalized like you capitalize the name of a whole country.

" 'Your Magical Magnificence'!" Bertha the Mouse read aloud. " 'The Master of the Granite Kingdom humbles himself to disturb you, the Keeper of all Secrets, with a sensitive matter...'

" 'At risk are The Royal Concerns, Duties and Privileges! At any moment His Majesty's subjects may find Lemon Drop Valley irresistible and therefore desert Granite Mountain! And to prevent that mega-catastrophe from coming to pass, the best course of action is to demagnetize the Coveted Path! This is exactly what your devoted servant, the Lord of the Granite Kingdom, respectfully asks of you'."

Then followed the signature, sealed by the Royal seal.

Bertha the Mouse had silenced herself, waiting for a signal from the Great wizard to continue. But already, Spark's attention was delivered by the unpleasant and even ominous sound of the word, "demagnetize" ringing through his skull.

After all, as soon as the Coveted Path was demagnetized, all his dreams would come to an end.

He would never (do you understand?), NEVER smell these magnificent flowers, see these two moons, speak to the stone monument or lay his eyes on the delightful Stella! Instead, he would be bound to remain a stonemason, just like all of the other dwellers of Granite Mountain.

"Well, can you offer an opinion on the matter, my dear Bertha?" the wizard Lestro said finally.

Oh, Bertha the Mouse could indeed. Moreover, she was all too eager to deliver it.

"I believe," she fired off, "the Coveted Path must be demagnetized. One can't allow the King to sacrifice the way of life he's been accustomed to since his childhood! I would never agree to part with my way of life! Absolutely not!"

It took Spark a great deal of effort to stop himself from screaming, "No, no, the Coveted Path can't be left without magnets! Don't you understand?"

But he learned that it sometimes pays to be a little patient and, when thinking back to this conversation later, he was pleased that he had been able to restrain himself.

For it so happened that the wizard Lestro's opinion almost coincided with his own. And, what's more, Spark couldn't even dream of speaking the thoughts as eloquently as did the wizard Lestro.

"You are right, dear Bertha," the wizard Lestro said in response. "But His Majesty's habits are based on privileges that require sacrifices not from him, but from all others. And if you take that into account, can you still call the end of the Royal way of life a sacrifice?"

"His Majesty isn't requiring sacrifices from others," retorted Bertha heatedly.

"Try to think of those who magnetized the Path in the first place…"

"You mean the Inventors? I don't think they are to be taken seriously."

"Think of the goal that they must have had in mind," the wizard Lestro continued, having turned a deaf ear to her comment, "I am personally inclined to believe that they wanted to open access to the Valley for the stonemasons. Where, if not in Lemon Drop Valley, could they learn how to build machines capable of liberating them from endlessly having to hew the cliffs with their pickaxes?"

"I thought the law forbade them from going down into the Valley," Bertha objected.

"Fortunately, no laws last forever!" the wizard Lestro responded and gestured to Bertha to continue reading.

Next was a letter from some Narcissus, who complained of some Volchaks ambushing Pyzhiks and Yushkas!

At first Spark didn't understand what that all was about. He was to encounter both Narcissus and the Volchaks no earlier than in our next book. But later it dawned on him that the ones who had been ambushed were not strangers at all, but Super-Pyzhik and Stella the Yushka.

But instead of making a move, he kept listening.

There was also a counter-complaint from the Volchaks.

"Narcissus infringes upon our freedom!" they wrote, wasting no time on compliments or greetings, "and instead of a fair fight, where the end result is unpredictable, he just fires at us with his rifle. What if he really hits someone? Consequently, his rifle must be seized, and Narcissus hung from a tree branch. Regards, General Volchak."

There was also a letter from the dwarf Zhabrey, complaining about both the Meduns and the brothers Klots. There was something from the Klots as well, but it was rather unclear what exactly they wrote. Being illiterate, the Klots had simply covered the entire page with Xs.

When the last letter had been read, the wizard Lestro asked Bertha to bring him his Flyer-Boots.

"The time has come to get to the bottom of all of this!" he announced.

Farewell to Bertha

All his magic boots were kept in a tower, near the room with Mash-fatum. There were all kinds of boots in that tower — the Fast-walkers, the Flyers, the Invisibles (of various styles), the Voice-changers, which allowed the wizard to speak in either falsetto or basso. There were so many different boots! You couldn't count them all!

But the wizard wouldn't be called the Great wizard were he not able to remember the purpose of each pair of boots. So he pretty much never got the boots mixed up! Although there was that one time when Lestro accidentally put on the Fast-walkers instead of the Sleepers.

As he ran around the bedroom, he marveled at the fact that he lost all of his desire to sleep. He ran all night long. The sun had already risen by the time it finally dawned on him that he had put on the wrong pair!

But that happened a long time ago, and there has been no other incident since then.

"Eighth shelf to the right!" called out Lestro, trying to help Bertha in her search.

As soon as the wizard put on his black hooded cloak, which resembled the wings of a bat (all wizards, as you well know, have such a cape), Bertha came back, carrying the right pair of boots.

She blew the dust off of them, and with a familiar movement (as she had done many times before), put them on the wizard's feet. Then Bertha stepped back, folding her hands over her belly.

Usually, the wizard barely had time to raise the wings of the cloak before the Flyer-boots snatched him up and lifted him with such speed that his head went

right through the ceiling. The roof had to be fixed every time. Eventually, he had learned how to control the boots so that he could fly out of the window. This time, however, something completely unexpected occurred. Instead of flying, the stubborn boots decided to limp around the room, jumping every once in a while.

Bertha the Mouse quietly giggled into her apron. After all, the wizard resembled an old hen that could barely walk, let alone fly.

Concerned, Lestro looked the boots over. The left one was hopelessly worn out.

"Dearest Bertha, I must trouble you one more time. Would you bring me another pair, preferably a good one?"

Bertha left and didn't show up for a very long time. Finally, she came back with a pair of Invisibles.

"These aren't in good shape anymore, either," she said, "and the soles of these have come off. Remember, last week, when you tried them on, you became invisible only to your waistline!"

She chuckled again and then added sympathetically: "May be one can glue or bind them together?"

Had poor Bertha known that in the book of wizard Regulations, specifically, in Paragraph 378, there was a certain note directly relevant to Lestro, she probably would have immediately begun to weep, which she actually did a little later.

That Paragraph stated that the life of a wizard lasts exactly as long as it takes for him to have worn twenty thousand pairs of boots and not a pair more!

Of course, in place of his dying wish, the wizard can request an extension.

But Lestro had followed one strict rule from the days of his youth: NEVER to use magic for his own benefit!

And since all twenty thousand pairs were already worn out (and this pair was the last of them), there were no doubts left.

"Well, it's time to die," calmly said Lestro, having checked the Book of Regulations one more time, just to be sure.

Oh, what these words did to poor Bertha! Weeping, she yanked off her pretty pink shoes (complete with white bows) and placed them by the wizards' feet.

"Don't die, oh, Illustrious-and-Powerful One! Take a pair of my shoes! They're almost new! And downstairs in a box I have a pair of brand new ones, with the label still on them!"

But Lestro only sighed and tenderly stroked Bertha's head.

Gentle Bertha... She didn't know, of course, that in the language of wizards, "to die" does not mean the same thing as it does in the language of ordinary people.

"Don't despair, Bertha! We'll meet again!" Lestro tried to calm her down. "Tomorrow you will go for a stroll in the Royal park. And I will fly above you in a shape of frigate called *The Silver Fleece*. I'll look at you from the misty heights, and you'll wave at me with your handkerchief!"

"For a stroll in the Royal park?" exclaimed the Mouse. "And what am I going to be doing there? No! I'll drown myself in tears and will fly after you... I'll become a flying mouse! After all, aren't there mice that know how to fly? No, I will never forget you!"

"Oh, but you will," said the wizard pensively. "I'd like to turn you into the duchess of white mice and marry you off to Sigismund the Tail-less."

"Sigismund the Tail-less!" was all that Bertha was able to utter as she tried to catch her breath, overwhelmed by the prospect.

"Hurry up, dear Bertha! There is a golden carriage waiting for you down below!"

And so Lestro was left alone in his enormous, desolate castle. Well, not quite alone, since Tonino and Spark were still there, and not so enormous, not anymore. As soon as he took his leave of the castle, the castle immediately began to shrink, its towers withering and falling.

To Part with the Valley for Good

Tonino and Spark were silently walking, knowing not where. Spark hastened his step, although there was no need to rush.

"I have gained some friends only to lose them at once... and I need to mourn alone!" he said as he strained to race ahead.

"But who are those friends who don't even know you?" asked Tonino, looking at Spark's back.

"Then what, do you think, I should call the Great wizard and Bertha the Mouse?" Spark replied heatedly.

"Bertha, for example, is a less-than-best friend. And now, when she turns into a queen, she'll stop thinking about friends altogether," Tonino said as he moved past Spark.

It was hard for him to believe that Spark could so casually, so callously exclude Tonino the confectioner from his list of friends... Should Tonino ever start to count his friends, it would turn out that he had fewer than two of them and certainly not more than one... So, he held on for the right moment to spell out his resentment.

Spark followed Tonino, brooding about Stella. Soon, she too will have no time to think of friends. And although he was eager to tell Tonino of their chance encounter on the seashore, the proper words somehow escaped him.

"I came down to the Valley to leave a trace of myself... Just think... I can erect a monument to them with my own hands!" Spark declared triumphantly.

"And who, exactly, are they?" Tonino mused.

"The Volchaks' victims, of course!" Spark replied, vexed at himself for bringing up the Yushka topic in such a clumsy way.

"But the Yushkas and the Pyzhiks, if that's who you are thinking of, are not yet victims of the Volchaks... And besides... you don't really know them either..." Tonino countered.

"I do know them! I can even describe the monument I'll make! Do you want to hear?"

Yes, Tonino did.

Imagine, on lemon-drop sand there is a captive Yushka. She seems to be asleep, but she is under a spell. And the witchcraft made her white hair go deep underground. To break the sorcery one has to comb her hair. But no one knows the secret of how...

"My poor Spark," Tonino exclaimed, "did you fall in love?"

"Stonemasons never fall in love," Spark fired back, burning of love. "And one thing's for sure, after having lost so much I have decided to part with the Valley for good."

Tonino stood dumbfounded. Could he ever have predicted such an ending?

"Well, why don't you say something?" Spark asked impatiently.

"You came down to us from your heights, like cat's pajamas," Tonino said, lowering his voice. "But if the wild idea ever strikes you to pay us a visit again, I mean, just in case, you might find this little something useful."

He pulled a tiny object out of his pocket and handed it to Spark.

What happens to our characters next, you will learn in the second book. Also, the author promises you that as soon as the book you hold in your hands has been read eighteen times, the new book will be waiting for you on the bedside table.

Contents

SCHEDULE OF OUR PUBLICATIONS

Spark, the Stone Man, First Series
February 2011 — Book One. Sand and Granite
August 2011 — Book Two. Historical Chronicles. The Inventors' Trace
February 2012 — Book Three. The Verdict
March 2012. — Announcing the Contest Terms for the best Animated Dream as
defined in our web site at: www.an-animation.com

Spark, the Stone Man, Second Series
September 2012 — Book Four
March 2013 — Book Five
September 2013 — Book Six
March 2013 — Announcing the Contest Results

SPARK THE STONE MAN
First Book of the First Series

PUBLICATION DATE: FEBRUARY 2011

PRINTED IN CHINA.
CPSIA Section 103 (a) Compliance:
www.beaconstar.com/consumer
ID: K0116490
Tracking No.: K0412177-7233

TECHNICAL DATA:
Trim pages: 8.5" x 11" Upright, 72 pp + case
Text: (4x4) color on 115 gsm matt paper
Ends: plain on 120 gsm wood free
Case: (4x4) color + film matt lamination on 128 gsm glossy over 2,5 mm board
Case bound: sewn in 16 pp, with separate glue ends, fully cased.

PRICE: $ U.S. 27

ISBN: 978-0-9828487-1-5
LCCN: 2010911130.

Pekasus
Factory of Animated Dreams

tel.: 1 (650) 681-9703 (in the U.S.), + 49 7632 823011 (in Germany),
+ 7 (499) 781-46-08 (in Moscow)
e-mail: Pekasus2011@gmail.com